Ignite Your Child's
Math Learning

PRSE
of the Book

"A heart-felt, wise, honest, and tender book. Enormously helpful for parents to enhance their children."

— Dr. Punit Sethi
Author of "International Business" and "Total Quality Management"

"Simple but profound. This is a book that encourages parents to help their children learn math."

— Mukesh Kulothia
Founder & Director of Muskurado.com and Author of "Move Mountain"

"This book opens your mind, broaden your mind, and strengthen you as nothing else can."

— Dr. B.S. Sharma (MD, Ph.D.)
Author of "Yoga — Yoga & Ayurveda for all"

This book is selected by National Book Trust(NBT), Government of India at:

▶ Cape Town Book Fair, 2012

▶ Sharjah International Book Fair, 2013

IGNITE
YOUR
CHILD'S
MATH LEARNING

A self-help Guide for the Parents to Make
their child a Mathematics Maestro

Worldwide Published by
Pendown Press

PENDOWN PRESS

An ISO 9001 & ISO 14001 Certified Co.,
Regd. Office: 2525/193, 1st Floor, Onkar Nagar-A,
Tri Nagar, Delhi-110035
Ph.: 09350849407, 09312235086
E-mail: info@pendownpress.com
Branch Office: 1A/2A, 20, Hari Sadan, Ansari Road,
Daryaganj, New Delhi-110002
Ph.: 011-45794768
Website: PendownPress.com

First Edition: 2019

ISBN: 978-93-81970-08-9

Contents

Few Words

Mathematics is an extremely important school subject. At school mathematics is usually taught in specific lessons, but children practice and use their mathematics throughout the school day.

As a parent, you are your child's first mathematics teacher. In fact, you have probably been doing math together since your child was very young. Counting pictures on a page and singing songs helped your child learn about numbers and counting. Building with objects such as blocks and cardboard boxes exposed your child to geometric ideas such as shape, size and symmetry. Chores such as putting away the dishes and sorting laundry engaged your child in sorting and categorizing, which are important features of data analysis.

Once your child enters school, it is important to continue to support their growing understanding of mathematics. There are many different ways to help your child learn and appreciate mathematics, even if math was not your favorite subject in school.

One of the most significant things parents can do is to help their children understand the normalcy and the value of struggle in mathematics. Learning math ultimately comes down to one thing: the ability, and choice, to put one's brain around a problem – to stare past the confusion, and struggle forward rather than flee.

This work will provide a helping hand to parents who are in need to understand their adolescent.

- Anita Verma

Acknowledgements

This edition of Ignite Your Child's Math Learning was made possible with the contributions of many people. I would like to acknowledge and pay special thanks to my husband Dinesh Verma and my daughter Tanya for their guidance in getting this book to print. A special thanks to Mr. Dinesh Verma for his valuable insights, critique, and constant support throughout the development of this publication.

Particular acknowledgment goes to Mr. Syed Makhdoom Ali (Editor). My thanks, also, to all of those who contributed their time, effort, and expertise to help produce this book.

I am indebted to the staff of the publisher (Pendown Press) for the important roles they played in helping to bring this book to print.

I am especially grateful to the cause of concern of parents towards their children in every walk of life.

- Anita Verma

INTRODUCTION

"Children must be taught how to think, not what to think."
~ *Margaret Mead*

What kind of attitude do you have towards math? Do you believe that math skills are more important job than life skills? Do you see math as useful in everyday life? Or do you dread doing things that involve math — figuring out how much new carpet you'll need, balancing the checkbook, reading the technical manual that came with the DVD player? How you answer these questions indicates how you may be influencing your child's attitudes towards math — and how he/she approaches learning math.

Although parents can be a positive force in helping children to learn math, they also can undermine their children's math ability and attitudes by saying things such as: "Math is hard," or "I'm not surprised you don't do well in math, I didn't like math either when I was in school," or "I wasn't very good in math and I'm a success, so don't worry about doing well." Although you can't make your child like math, you can encourage him/her to do so, and you can take steps to ensure that he/she learns to appreciate its value both in his/her everyday life and in preparing for his/her future. You might point out to him/her how fortunate he/she is to have the opportunity to learn mathematics today — when the knowledge of mathematics can open the door to so many interesting and exciting possibilities.

In everyday interactions with children, there are many things that parents can do — and do without lecturing or applying pressure — to help children in learning how to solve problems, to communicate mathematically and to demonstrate reasoning abilities. These skills are fundamental to learning mathematics.

Let's look closely at what it means to be a problem solver, to communicate mathematically and to demonstrate mathematical reasoning ability.

A problem solver is someone who questions, finds, investigates, and explores solutions to problems; demonstrates the ability to stick with a problem to find a solution; understands that there may be different ways to arrive at an answer; and applies math successfully to everyday situations. You can encourage your child to be a good problem solver by including him/her in routine activities that involve math — for example, measuring, weighing, figuring costs, and comparing prices of things he/she wants to buy.

To communicate mathematically means to use mathematical language, numbers, charts or symbols to explain things and to explain the reasoning for solving a problem in a certain way, rather than just giving the answer. It also means careful listening to understand others' ways of thinking and reasoning. You can help your child in learning how to communicate mathematically by asking him/her to explain what he/she must do to solve a math problem or how he/she arrived at his/her answer. You could ask your child to draw a picture or diagram to show how he/she arrived at the answer.

Mathematical reasoning ability means thinking logically, being able to see similarities and differences in objects or problems, making choices based on those differences and thinking about relationships among things. You can encourage your child's mathematical reasoning ability by talking frequently with him/her about these thought processes.

Some Important Things your Child Needs to Know about Mathematics

You can help your child to learn math by offering his/her insights into how to approach math. He/she will develop more confidence in his/her math ability if he/she understands the following points:

1. Problems Can be Solved In Different Ways

Although most math problems have only one answer, there may be many ways to get to that answer. Learning math is more than finding the correct answer; it's also a process of solving problems and applying what you've learned to new problems.

2. Wrong Answers Sometimes can be Useful

Ask your child to explain how he/she solved a math problem. His/her explanation might help you to discover if he/she needs help with number skills, such as addition, subtraction, multiplication, and division, or with the concepts involved in solving the problem.

3. Take Risks!

Help your child to be a risk taker. Help him/her see the

value of trying to solve a problem, even if it's difficult. Give your child time to explore different approaches to solving a difficult problem. As he/she works, encourage him/her to talk about what he/she is thinking. This will help him/her to strengthen math skills and to become an independent thinker and problem solver.

4. Being Able to do Mathematics In your Head Is Important

Mathematics isn't restricted to pencil and paper activities. Doing math "in your head" (mental math) is a valuable skill that comes in handy as we make quick calculations of costs in stores, restaurants, or petrol pump. Let your child know that by using mental math, his/her math skills will become stronger.

5. It's Sometimes OK to Use a Calculator to Solve Mathematics' Problems

It's OK to use calculators to solve math problems — sometimes. They are widely used today, and knowing how to use them correctly is important. The idea is for your child not to fall back on the excuse, "I don't need to know math — I've got a calculator." Let your child know that to use calculators correctly and most efficiently, he/she will need a strong grounding in math operations — otherwise, how will he/she know whether the answer he/she sees displayed is reasonable!

How to Use this Book?

The major portion of this book is made up of activities

that you can use with your child to strengthen math skills and build strong positive attitudes towards math. You don't need to be a great mathematician or to have a college degree in math to use them. Your time and interest and the pleasure that you share with your child as part of working together are what matter most.

As the activities pertain to specific mathematical concepts, the book provides a glossary defining these concepts. Also, at the end of this book, you'll find lists of resources, such as books for you and for your child, helpful Websites that you can open for more information about how to help your child with math. Let's get started!

x x x

"If you are a parent open doors to unknown directions to the child so he can explore. Don't make him afraid of the unknown, give his support."
~Osho

ACTIVITIES

"There is no job more important than parenting. This
I believe."
~Ben Carson

The activities in this section are arranged into four
categories: Mathematics in the Home, Mathematics
at the Grocery Store, Mathematics on the Go and
Mathematics for the Fun of It. For each activity, you'll
see a grade span — from pre-school through grade 5 —
that suggests when children should be ready to try it. Of
course, children don't always become interested in or
learn the same things at the same time. And they don't
suddenly stop enjoying one thing and start enjoying
another just because they are a little older. You're the best
judge of which activity your child is ready to try. For
example, you may find that an activity listed for children
in grades 1 or 2 works well with your pre-schooler. On

the other hand, you might discover that the same activity may not interest your child until he/she is in grade 3 or 4.

Feel free to make changes in an activity — shorten or lengthen it — to suit your child's interests and attention span. Most of the things that you might need for these activities are found around most homes.

As a parent, you can help your child learn in a way no one else can. That desire to learn is a key to your child's success, and, of course, enjoyment is an important motivator for learning. As you choose activities to use with your child, remember that helping him/her to learn doesn't mean that you can't laugh and have a good time. In fact, you can teach your child a lot through play. And you can play with and make games out of almost any math skill or concept. I hope that you and your child enjoy these activities and that they inspire you to think of additional activities of your own.

x x x

"Encourage and support your kids because children are apt to live up to what you believe of them."

MATHEMATICS IN THE HOME

"I am always trying to evolve, so I like to read
parenting books and things like that."
~Kourtney Kardashian

Your home is a great place for you to begin to explore and "talk" mathematics with your child. Incorporating math activities and language into familiar daily routines will show your child how math works in his/her everyday life and provide him/her with a safe environment in which he can take risks by trying new things.

1. Rhyme and Sing

Pre-school

Young children love to hear, sing and say nursery rhymes and songs. Counting rhymes and songs can be both enjoyable for them and introduce them to basic mathematics concepts, such as number names and number sequence.

What Parents Need?

- Book of nursery rhymes or songs
- Feather

What Can Parents Do?

- Teach your child the following counting rhyme:

    Four Little Ducks

    Four little ducks that I once knew,

    Fat ducks, skinny ducks, they were, too.

    But one little duck with a feather on his/her back,

    She ruled the others with a quack! quack! quack!

    Down to the river they all would go,

    1, 2, 3, 4, all in a row.

    But one little duck with a feather on his/her back,

    She ruled the others with a quack! quack! quack!

Say the rhyme with your child several times. When he/she can say the rhyme all the way through, have other family members join you. Give your child a feather and have his/her lead everyone around the room as you all sing.

- For the following rhyme, show your child how to perform the actions indicated.

Five Little Speckled Frogs

Five little speckled frogs

> *(hold up five fingers)*

Sitting on a speckled log

> *(sit on your heels)*

Eating some most delicious bugs

> *(pretend to eat)*

Yum! Yum!

One jumped into the pool

> *(jump)*

Where it was nice and cool

> *(cross arms over chest and shiver)*

Now there are four little speckled frogs.

> *(hold up four fingers)*

Burr-ump!

> *(Continue until no frogs are left.)*

After saying the rhyme, ask your child to hold up the correct number of fingers to show how many frogs are in the rhyme at the beginning. Then have him/her hold up the correct number of fingers and count to five with you as you say each numeral.

- Teach your child any counting rhymes and songs that were your personal favourites when you were a child, or have your child ask his/her grandparents what rhymes they knew when they were children. Other counting rhymes, songs, and games that you may want to teach your child include "One, Two, Buckle My Shoe," "This Old Man," "Ten in a Bed (Roll Over)" and "One for the Money."

2. Number Hunt

Pre-school

By counting, using number names and learning to recognize differences in number values, children build a foundation for the development of number sense and mathematical reasoning.

What Parents Need?

- 3 plastic eggs that come apart (or similar containers)

- Buttons

- Plastic netting

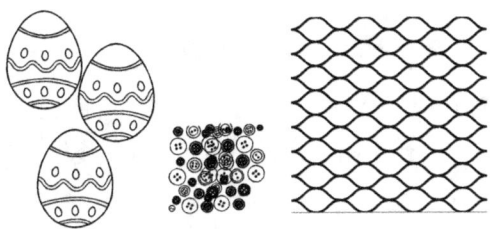

What Can Parents Do?

- In pieces of netting, loosely wrap different numbers of buttons and place one bag of buttons in each egg. With your child out of the room, hide the eggs.

- Call your child into the room and tell him that you've hidden three eggs and that you want him/her to find them. As he/she finds each egg, have his/her count aloud — "1," "2," "3."

- When he/she's found all the eggs, have him/her open each one and take out the bag of buttons (but not open it). Ask him/her to count how many buttons are in each bag.

Sometimes younger children don't understand that counting means naming numbers in a specific order. This simple point should be reinforced often.

3. Walk and Count

Pre-school - Kindergarten

Ordinary activities can be used to reinforce young children's number sense and introduce them to arithmetic operations, such as addition and subtraction.

What Can Parents Do?

- Take your child for a walk. You can walk around your neighbourhood, through a park, or just around the rooms in your home. As you walk, say silly things for him/her to do, such as the following:

  - Take two big steps and three little steps.

  - Take three little steps, hop one time, take three big steps.

  - Take one little step, turn around two times.

  - Hop four times, turn around one time.

  - Take three big steps forward and two big steps backward.

- Count aloud each kind of action that your child performs and compliment him/her for his/her efforts — "1, 2—1, 2, 3—1, 2. That's great!"

- Let your child turn the tables and say silly things for you to do as you walk.

- For your kindergarten child, expand the activity by asking him/her to "guess" (estimate) how many of his/her steps it will take, for example, to get from the tree to the corner. After he/she makes his/her estimate, have him/her count steps to see how close the estimate is. Next ask him/her how many of your steps it will take. Will it take you more steps or fewer to go the same distance? Again, have him/her count to see if his/her answers are correct.

Throughout the day, find ways to let children practice using arithmetic skills. Ask, for example, "How many magazines came by the post?" "How many more letters will we need to get to have 10 letters?" "Which are there more of, magazines or letters?"

4. Find It

Pre-school - Kindergarten

Young children may not recognize that numbers are all around them. Pointing out numbers on everyday items increases their number sense.

What Parents Need?

- Boxes, cans, bottles of food and other household supplies

What Can Parents Do?

- Place several boxes, cans, and bottles on the kitchen table. You might use a cereal box, a can of soup and a bottle of dishwashing soap. Sit with your child and point out one or two numbers on each item. (Numbers can be found in the names of some products, as well as in the list of contents and in addresses. However, rather than pointing to a very large number, such as a PIN code, point to one digit in that code — (6 or 3 or 8).

- Point to one of the items and say a number that is easy to see. Ask your child to find it. Then have him/her look for that number on the other items.

- Have your child choose a number for you to find on one of the containers.

Calling attention to numbers that are all around them lets children know that numbers are important and that they are used for many different purposes.

5. Sort It Out

Pre-school - Kindergarten

Sorting and matching activities introduce young children to many mathematical operations, including classification and measurement.

What Parents Need?

- Pairs of socks of different sizes and colours
- Laundry

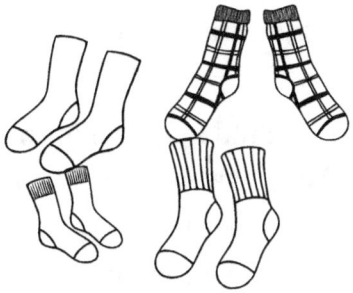

What Can Parents Do?

- When you're sorting and folding clean laundry, have your child join you and do such things as the following:

  - Hold up a pair of matching socks that belong to him/her and say, for example, "These socks go together because each sock is red and each one fits the same size foot — yours!"

  - Pick up another sock and ask your child to look through the pile for the sock that matches it. When he/she chooses a sock, have his/her tell you how he/she knows that it's the right one.

  - Continue holding up socks until your child has paired them all. If he/she mispairs any socks, gently correct him/her by asking him/her to tell the colour of each sock and to put the socks together to see if they are the same size.

  - After you've done this activity several times, let your child choose the socks for you to pair. (Occasionally choose a wrong sock to give his/

her the chance to help you correct your mistake!).

- Have your child help you in sorting the laundry to be washed. Ask her, for example, to put all the blue things together, all the whites, all the towels, and so forth. You might also have his/her count as he/she sorts. How many towels are there? How many shirts? Try saying, "I count five shirts. Is that right?" Then have your child count aloud the number of shirts. From time to time, give an incorrect number so that he/she can count the items one by one and show you that you've made a mistake.

Children need to see that grown-ups also make math mistakes occasionally to identify their mistakes and find ways to correct them.

6. Shape Up

Pre-school - Kindergarten

Using objects that are familiar to young children can be a good way to introduce them to differences in shapes and to classification.

What Parents Need?

- Snack crackers in the shape of circles, squares, triangles.

- Bread to cut into different shapes.

What Can Parents Do?

Here are some simple things that you can do to focus your child's attention on different shapes:

- Fill a bowl with snack crackers in shapes such as circles, triangles, and squares. Point to a cracker and say, for example, "Look, this one's round. This one has three sides. See, 1-2-3. This one has four sides. Let's count them — 1-2-3-4." Place a circular cracker on the table and ask your child to find other crackers that have the same shape. Continue with the other shapes.

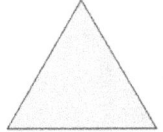  

- As you make sandwiches, cut the bread into circles, squares, and triangles so that you have two each of same shape. Ask your child to match the pairs of shapes to make Shape Sandwiches.

- Have your child search for and point out different shapes on his/her clothes or in the room.

Playing with children can provide many opportunities to engage in activities such as sorting, matching, comparing, and arranging.

7. A-Weigh We Go!

Grade 1

Observing, estimating, weighing, and comparing are all essential mathematics skills.

What Parents Need?

- Bathroom or kitchen scales

- Objects to weigh, such as bags of sugar, flour, potatoes or onions; boxes of detergent and cookies; shoes of different sizes

- Paper and pencil

- A small plastic zipper bag filled with sugar and much larger zipper bag filled with cornflakes (or popped popcorn)

- Suitcase

What Can Parents Do?

- Show your child two objects, such as a five kilogram bag of sugar and a ten kilogram bag of potatoes, and ask him/her to guess which weighs more. Show him/her how to use a scale to weigh the objects and see if his/her guess is right or wrong.

- Next show him/her several objects and ask him/her to guess how much each weighs. Have him/her write his/her estimates, then weigh the objects to see if they're correct.

- If you choose, have your child estimate his/her own weight, as well as that of other family members, and use the bathroom scale to check his/her guesses.

- Extend the activity or make it more challenging by doing the following:

  - Show your child the small plastic bag filled with sugar and the larger bag filled with cornflakes or popped popcorn. Ask your child which will weigh more, the smaller or the larger bag? Have him/her weigh the bags to check whether his/her guess is correct. Afterwards, point out that bigger does not always mean heavier.

  - Ask your child how he/she can weigh a suitcase that is too large to fit on the bathroom scale. Listen carefully to his/her answers — try some of his/her suggestions, if possible — and praise him/her for learning to think through problems. If he/she doesn't come up with a solution, show him/her that one way to find the weight of the suitcase is for him/her to stand on the scales while holding it and noting the total weight. Then put the suitcase aside and weigh him/her again and note his/her weight. If he/she subtracts his/her weight from the total weight, the answer is the weight of the suitcase.

Using simple bathroom and kitchen scales at home prepares children for using equipment in school to weigh and measure.

8. Coins and Notes

Grade 1

Activities that involve money are a good way to develop mathematical reasoning and to reinforce what children are learning in school about numbers and arithmetic operations, such as addition and subtraction.

What Parents Need?

- Dice

- One rupee coins, five rupee coins, ten rupee note.

What Can Parents Do?

This is a good game to play with the family.

- Have each player roll the dice and say the number. Then give the player that number of one rupee coins. Explain that each coin is worth one rupee.

- When a player gets 5 one rupee coins, replace the coins with a five rupee coin. Explain that 5 one rupee coins have the same value as 1 five rupee coin. When he/she gets 5 more one rupee coins, replace the one rupee coins and a five rupee coin with a ten rupee note. Help him/her to see that the value of 5 one rupee coins plus the value of a five rupee coin equals ten rupees, which is the value of a ten rupee note.

- The first player to reach a set amount — 25 or 50 rupees, for example — wins.

Children can be confused by money. Some might think that the larger a coin is, the more valuable it is.

9. Treasure Hunt

Grade 1

Once children begin school, math-related activities at home they become able to reinforce what they are learning about numbers and arithmetic operations such as addition and subtraction, as well as reinforce classification skills and mathematical reasoning.

What Parents Need?

- Large container
- Buttons, bottle caps, old keys, or any other small item that you can count.

What Can Parents Do?

- As a rainy day activity, place the items in the container and give it to your child. Have him/her sort and classify items into piles: keys, buttons, and so forth. Then have him/her to explain how the items in each pile are alike and how they are different. For example, some buttons may be big and some small; some keys may be silver coloured and some gold-coloured.

- Have your child choose one of the piles and organize the items in it by one characteristic, such as length. Have him/her lay the items end to end then compare and contrast what he/she sees. For example, how many short keys? long keys?

- Next, ask your child to use the items in another pile of items to solve simple math problems. Try problems such as the following:

  - If you have 10 bottle caps and give me two, how many bottle caps will be left with you?

  - If you have three big buttons and three small ones, how many buttons do you have altogether?

- Create activities that challenge your child to use mathematical reasoning. Ask him/her, for example, to look closely at items and answer questions such as the following:

  - Is a gold-coloured key always heavier than a silver-coloured one?

- Do the big buttons always have more holes than the smaller ones?

Keeping the tone of math activities light will increase the likelihood that children will want to do them and make the activities seem less like "homework".

10. In the Newspaper

Grade 1

Newspapers are good resources for building number sense and arithmetic skills and using mathematical reasoning.

What Parents Need?

- Newspaper
- Safety scissors
- Pencil or crayon
- Glue
- Paper
- Hole puncher
- Yarn

What Can Parents Do?

- Give your child a newspaper and a set of numbers to look for — for example, from 1 to 25 (or 1 to 100 if he/she is familiar with the higher numbers). Have him/her cut out the numbers and glue them in numerical order onto a large piece of paper. Call his/her attention to any ways in which the numbers differ — for example, some will be in a bigger size of type than others, some will be in bold or italic type. Have him/her read the numbers to you, then put the paper aside. Have him/her practice counting up to that number then counting down from it. Also try having him/her count to the number by 2s or 5s.

- Next, have your child make a counting book by using pictures he/she's cut from the newspaper. Have him/her write the page numbers at the bottom of each blank page and paste one item on page 1, two on page 2 and so forth. Explain that all of the things he/she puts on a page must be alike in some way — all animals, all cricket players, all cars, and so on. Help him/her to write the name of the items on the appropriate page.

- Have your child read the book to you. Afterwards, ask him/her questions such as the following:

  - How many pictures did you cut out altogether *(1+2+...+10)?*

- How many total pictures are on pages 1-3? on pages 1-6?

- We know that 6 = 2 x 3. Are there twice as many pictures on page 6 as on page 3?

- Are there twice as many pictures from page 1 to 6 as from pages 1 to 3?

- Which are there more of: pictures on pages 2, 3, and 4, or pictures on pages 5 and 6?

Newspapers also can be used to help young children learn to recognize numbers in different sizes and kinds of type and to understand that the way a number looks does not change its value.

11. Fill It Up

Grades 1-2

Filling empty containers provides opportunities to explore geometric concepts, such as "more or less" and volume, and to apply measurement skills.

What Parents Need?

- Measuring cup
- Four large glasses of equal size and shape
- Water

What Can Parents Do?

- On a table, put the glasses in a row and fill them with water as follows: 1/3 cup, 1/2 cup, 3/4 cup, 1 cup. Ask your child questions that encourage him/her to compare, estimate and think about measurement. Ask, for example, "Which glass has more water? Which has less?"

- Pour more water into one of the glasses to make it equal to the amount of water in another glass. Move the glasses around so that the glasses that have the same amount of water are not next to each other. Ask your child to find the glasses that have the same amount of water.

- Help your child to do math in his/her head. Ask questions such as, "If I have four cups of water and I need seven, how many more do I need to pour?"

As you use measuring cups, call attention to the different levels and use their names: "one-fourth," "one-half", and so on. This will begin to familiarize children with the language they will use when they begin to work with fractions.

12. Tracking Time

Grades 2-3

Introducing children to statistics and data analysis can begin by having them collect information, analyze it and describe or present their findings in an organized way.

What Parents Need?

- Stopwatch, watch or clock
- Newspaper
- Blank paper
- Graph paper
- Ruler
- Small round object to trace to make a pie chart
- Pencil and markers or crayons

What Can Parents Do?

- Show your child how to keep track of the time he/she spends on two activities, such as watching television and doing homework. Help him/her to make a chart with two columns, one labeled "Television" and one labeled "Homework." Down the left side of the chart, write the days of the week. Tell him/her that you want him/her to write the number of minutes he/she spends doing each activity on each day. At the end of the week, sit down with him/her and talk about what the table shows.

- Help your child to make a chart to use as he/she watches television. Give him/her a stopwatch (or an easy-to-read clock or watch) and tell him/her to record how much time of each television show is used for commercials and how much time is used for the actual show. Have him/her keep the record for one night of viewing. On the graph paper, help him/her to make a bar graph that shows the different amounts of time devoted to the show and to commercials. Or, show him/her how to make a pie chart.

- Together with your child, keep track of how he/she spends time in one 24-hour period: time spent on sleeping, eating, playing, reading, and going to school. Help him/her to measure a strip of paper 24 inches long, with each inch representing one hour. Using a different colour for each activity, have him/her colour the number of hours he/she spends in each activity. You and other family members can make similar charts; then your child can compare the charts and see how everyone in the family spends time.

A good way to show children how statistics are used in the "real world" is to call their attention to statistical charts in newspapers and magazines and talk with them about what the charts show and why this information is important.

13. Fraction Action

Grades 2-3

In introducing children to the concept of *fractions* —
numbers that aren't whole numbers (such as 1/2, 1/3 and
1/4) — it's often a good idea to use objects that they can see
and touch.

What Parents Need?

- Large clear container (holding at least 2 cups)
- Masking tape
- Marker
- Measuring cups (1/2, 1/3 or 1/4 cup measure)
- Unpopped popcorn

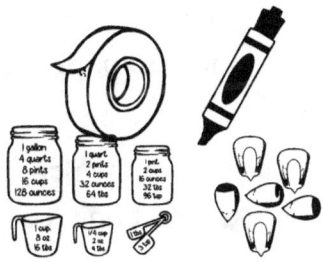

What Can Parents Do?

- Invite your child to help you in making popcorn
  for the family. Begin by having him/her put a
  piece of masking tape from top to bottom on one
  side of the large container.

- For younger children, use a 1/2 cup measure. For
  older children, use a 1/3 or 1/4 cup measure.

Choose the unit of measure and fill the measuring cup with popcorn. Give the cup to your child and ask him/her questions such as the following:

- How many whole cups do you think the container will hold?

- How many 1/2 cups (or 1/3 cups or 1/4 cups) do you think it will hold?

• Let your child pour the measured popcorn into the clear container. Have him/her continue to pour the same amount into the container until it is full. As he/she pours each equal amount, have him/her mark the level on the container by drawing a line on the tape. Then have him/her write the fraction, corresponding to the unit of measure on the line. After the container is full, have your child count up the total number of cup increments (1/2, 1/3 or 1/4) and compare it to his/her estimate from above.

• As you measure out the popcorn to pop, ask your child to answer questions such as the following:

- How many 1/2 cups equal a cup? Two cups.

- How many 1/4 cups equal 1/2 cup? Two cups.

• Pop the corn and enjoy!

Children may reasonably want to say, for example, that 1/4 cup plus 1/4 cup makes 2/4 cups. Letting them work with measuring cups or other measuring devices can let them see that 2/4 is the same as 1/2.

14. Simply Symmetrical

Grades 3-5

A shape is symmetrical if it can be cut along a straight line into two halves that are mirror images of each other. Learning about symmetry gives children a good sense of geometric principles and calls on their mathematical reasoning abilities.

What Parents Need?

- Shapes such as a circle, a square, and a rectangle, cut from heavy paper

- Sheets of paper (rectangular)

- Pencil, marker or crayon

- Magazine pictures of symmetrical objects

- Safety scissors

- Glue

What Can Parents Do?

- As your child watches, show him/her the square that you've made. Fold it in half and show him/her that the two parts are exactly alike — or *symmetrical*. Do the same with the circle and the rectangle. Then give the shapes to your child and ask him/her to make the folds him/herself. Extend the activity by having him/her do the following:

  - Find as many ways as he/she can to fold half of the square onto the other half. *(There are four ways: two diagonals and two lines "down the middle").*

- Do the same for the rectangle. *(There are only two ways: down the middle of the long side, then down the middle of the short side. In going from a square to a rectangle, the diagonals are lost as lines of symmetry).*

- Do the same with the circle. *(Circles can fold along any diameter. Use this discovery to introduce your child to the word "diameter" — the length of a straight line that passes through the center of a circle).*

- Ask him/her to find the center of a circle by folding it in half twice. *(He/she'll discover that any diameter — line of folding in half — passes through the center of the circle, an activity that will prepare him/her for understanding more complicated geometry later on).*

- Show your child a rectangular piece of paper. Ask her, "What shape will you get if you fold this piece of paper in half?" Have him/her fold the paper, then ask, "Did you get a square or another rectangle?" Using scissors to cut the paper, show him/her that a rectangle will fold to a square only if it is twice as long as it is wide.

- Fold a sheet of paper in half lengthwise. Have your child draw half of a circle, heart or butterfly from top to bottom along the fold on each side of the paper. Have him/her cut out the shapes that were drawn. Unfold the paper to see the symmetrical figure.

- Cut out a magazine picture of something that is symmetrical (try, for example, a basketball or a computer screen). Cut it down the center (the line of symmetry). Glue one half of the picture on the paper. Ask your child to draw the missing half.

- With your child, explore your house for symmetrical designs — things that have equal sides. Ask your child how many he/she can find. Tell him/her to look at wallpaper, floor tiles, pictures, bedspreads, and appliances.

- Have your child print the alphabet. Then ask him/her to find a letter that has only one line of symmetry — only one way to be divided in half. (*B has one.*) Ask him/her to find a letter that has two lines of symmetry — two ways to be divided in half. (*H has two.*) Ask which letters look the same when they're turned upside down? (*H, I, N, O, S, X and Z*).

✗ ✗ ✗

MATHEMATICS AT THE GROCERY STORE

"I am always trying to evolve, so I like to read parenting books and things like that."
~Kourtney Kardashian

The grocery store is one of the best examples of a place where the ability to use mathematics is put to work in the "real world." It's a great place to practice measurement and estimation and to learn about volume and quantity and their relationships to the sizes and shapes of containers — geometry!

1. One Potato, Two Potatoes

Pre-school

Making a grocery shopping list can be both enjoyable and an opportunity to reinforce young children's number sense.

What Parents Need?

- List of grocery items

- Colour pictures of grocery items cut from magazines, catalogs or advertising flyers (for example, choose pictures of different kinds of vegetables, fruit, containers of milk or juice, cans of soup, boxes of cereal and crackers, loaves of bread)

- Index cards (or similar-sized cards cut from heavy paper)

- Glue stick

- Small box (large enough to hold the cards)

What Can Parents Do?

- Put together the set of food pictures and help your child paste each picture onto a card. Then have your child sit with you as you make up a grocery shopping list. Read the list aloud to her, item by item, saying, for example, "We need to buy milk. Find the picture of the milk." When the child finds the picture, have him/her put it in the box.

Continue through the list, asking him/her to find pictures of such things as apples, potatoes, bread, soup, and juice.

- When you've finished, ask your child to tell you how many things you need to buy; then help him/her to count the pictures in the box.

- Ask your child to put all the pictures of vegetables in one group, then all the pictures of fruit in another group. (You might continue with items that are in cans, items that are in boxes, and so on).

- Point to one group of pictures, such as the fruit. Help him/her to count the number of pictures in that group. Have him/her do the same for other groups.

Use advertising flayers or newspaper advertisements to help your child identify, classify and count items. Ask, for example, "How many cans of soup are there?" "What vegetables do you see?" and so forth.

2. Ready, Set, Shop!

Grade 1

Grocery shopping offers opportunities to let children apply a range of mathematics skills, including data collection and estimation.

What Parents Need?

- Pencil and paper
- Calculator

What Can Parents Do?

- To help your child learn about collecting data, involve him/her in making a shopping list for a special occasion, such as his/her birthday party. As you discuss what you need to buy, write out a list of grocery items. Then review the list with your child and tell him/her to make a check mark next to each item that you name. If you need more than one of an item, such as cartons of ice cream, tell him/her how many checks to make beside that item. Review the list with him/her and have him/her tell you what items — and how many of each that you need to buy.

- Ask your child to choose something that he/she wants for dinner — a cake, a salad, pizza. Have him/her check to see what ingredients you already have; then ask him/her to help you make a shopping list. At the grocery store, let him/her find each item on the list. Help him/her to compare prices for different brands of the same items (such as boxes of cake mix) to see which items are the best buys.

- Ask your child questions such as, "Which is cheaper, this package of two tomatoes for ₹1.50 or three of these tomatoes at 60 paisa each?" Have him/her estimate, then check his/her answer with a calculator.

Using the advertised prices in a newspaper to estimate the cost of items on a shopping list can help children sharpen their mental math and estimation abilities.

3. Get Into Shapes

Grade 1

Introducing children to geometric principles can be as simple as helping them recognize how different shapes are used in common settings.

What Can Parents Do?

- At the store, ask your child questions to focus his/her attention on the shapes that you see. Ask him/her to find, for example, items that have circles or triangles on them or boxes that are in the form of a cube or a rectangular solid.

- As you shop, point out shapes of products — rolls of paper towels, unusually shaped bottles, cookie boxes shaped like houses. Talk with your child about the shapes. Ask him/her why he/she thinks products, such as paper towels and packages of napkins, come in different shapes. Have him/her notice which shapes stack easily. Try to find a stack of products that looks like a pyramid.

- Ask your child for reasons the shapes of products and packages are important to store owners. *(Some shapes stack more easily than others and can save space).*

Before shopping tries, review different shapes with children by pointing them out in items around the house. Encourage them to use the correct name for each shape: square, rectangle, triangle, circle, cube, cylinder, and so forth.

4. Clip and Save

Grades 1-2

Discount coupons can be used to help children learn the value of money as well as to let them show off their addition and subtraction skills.

What Parents Need?

- Coins of one rupee, two rupee, five rupee, and ten rupee

- Grocery store discount coupons

- Pencil and paper

What Can Parents Do?

- Show your child a grocery store discount coupon for a product that he/she likes to eat and have him/her count out coins to show how much money the discount coupon saves on the product. For example, if the coupon is for 30 rupees off a jar of peanut butter, give your child two rupee coins and five rupee coins and tell him/her to count out thirty rupees or 6 five rupee coins. Give your child all the coins and challenge him/her to figure out how many different coin combinations he/she can make to total 30 rupees.

- Ask your child how much money you can save with two or three 20 rupee discount coupons. Show him/her the other discount coupons and ask him/her how much money could be saved with each one. Have him/her write the amounts and then add them to show how much could be saved if all the discount coupons were used.

Help children feel that they're a part of family budgeting by encouraging them to look in newspapers and flyers for discount coupons for items that the family uses. Have them look for discount coupons for items that they want to buy with allowance or birthday money.

5. Weighing In

Grades 3-4

Grocery shopping offers opportunities for children to increase their estimation and measurement skills by choosing and weighing fruit and vegetables.

What Parents Need?

- A grocery scale

What Can Parents Do?

- In the produce section of the store, explain to your child that what you pay for fruit and vegetables is based, in large part, on the quantity you buy and what it weighs — that produce is usually sold for a certain amount per kilogram. Tell him/her that kilograms are divided into smaller parts called 'grams', and it takes 1000 grams to make one kilogram. Show him/her the scale that is used to weigh produce.

- Gather the products you want to buy and ask your child to weigh a few items. Then have him/her estimate the weight of another item before he/she weighs it. If you need one kilogram of apples, ask him/her to place several apples on the scale and then estimate how many apples he/she will have to add or take away to make one kilogram.

- Let your child choose two pieces of fruit, such as oranges. Have him/her hold one piece in each hand and guess which weighs more. Then have him/her use the scale to see if he/she is right.

- Ask your child questions such as the following to encourage him/her to think about measurement and estimation:

  - Will six potatoes weigh more or less than six oranges?

  - Which has more potatoes, a kilogram of big ones or a kilogram of little ones?

  - How much do potatoes cost for each kilogram? If they cost 10 rupees per kilogram, what is the total cost of the six potatoes?

- If your child knows the metric system (and the scale has a metric range), have him/her weigh items in grams and kilograms. Ask him/her to find out the following:

- How a gram compares to a kilogram.

- How many grams an apple weighs.

- How many kilograms (or kilograms plus grams) a sack of potatoes weighs.

- Which contains more apples, 500 grams or one kilogram?

- Which weighs more, 500 grams of apples or one kilogram of apples?

In many schools, children learn the metric system of metres, grams and litres, along with the more familiar system of feet, kilograms and gallons. Practicing measurement in both ways help children to learn both systems.

6. Check It Out

Grades 3-4

The checkout lane of a grocery store can be a good place for children to practice using mental math by estimating the cost of groceries and figuring out change.

What Can Parents Do?

- As you wait in a grocery checkout lane, use the time to have your child estimate what the total cost of your groceries will be. Tell him/her that one easy way to estimate a total is to round off numbers. That is, if an item costs 98 rupees, round it off to 100 rupees. Explain that the answer he/she gets won't be the exact cost, but it will be *about* that. Tell him/her that the word *about* shows that the amount you say is just an estimate.

- Using the estimated total, ask your child: "If the groceries cost 16 rupees and I have a 20 rupees bill, how much change should the checker give back to me? If the cost is 17 rupees, what coins is he/she likely to give me?

- At the checkout counter, ask your child to watch as the items are rung up. What's the actual total cost of the groceries? How does this amount compare to the estimate? When you pay for the items, will you get change back from your 20 rupees bill, or will you have to give the checker more money?

- If you receive change, have your child count it to make sure the amount is correct.

Grocery shopping can be a good place to show children a practical use for calculators — for example, as a way to keep a running total of what the groceries cost.

7. Put It Away

Grades 1-5

Putting away groceries help children to develop their classifying and mathematical reasoning skills and the ability to analyze data.

What Parents Need?

- Groceries

What Can Parents Do?

- Make a game out of putting away groceries. As you empty the bags, group the items according to some common features. You might, for example, put together all the items that go in the refrigerator or all the items in cans.

- Tell your child that you're going to play "Guess My Rule." Explain that in this game, you sort the items and she has to guess what rule you used for grouping the items.

- After your child catches on to the game, reverse roles and ask him/her to use another "rule" to group these same items. She might, for example, group the refrigerator items into those that are in glass bottles or jars and those in other kinds of packaging. She might group the cans into those with vegetables, those with fruit and those with soup. When she's regrouped the items, guess what rule she used.

Children can often make up very creative rules for classifying things. Don't be surprised if you have trouble guessing your child's rule!

✗ ✗ ✗

"The voice of parents is the voice of gods, for to their children they are heaven's lieutenants."   ~William Shakespeare

MATHEMATICS ON THE GO

"The moment a child is born, the mother is also born.
She never existed before."
~Osho

Most of us spend a lot of time moving from place to place in our cars or in cabs, on buses and on trains and in airplanes. Travelling, whether across country or around the world, provides many opportunities for you to help your child learn about and apply math.

1. Off We Go

Pre-school

Involving young children in trip planning can be a time to introduce them to measuring and comparing.

What Parents Need?

- Maps
- Marker

What Can Parents Do?

- Before your family leaves on a trip, sit with your child and show him a map that includes both where you live and where you're going. Talk with him about what maps are and how they are used. Use the marker to circle your hometown and then explain that this is where you live. Then circle the place you plan to visit and explain that this is where you're going. Draw a line between the two (a simple straight line —don't attempt to follow the highway route).

- Point out and mark other places that have meaning for your child — the place where his grandmother lives, the place where his favourite theme park is located and so forth, and do some simple comparisons of distance: "Grandma is closer to us than where we're going on vacation. See. She lives here and where we're going is way over here." The idea is to familiarize your child with maps and distances, not to have him understand complicated directions or measurements.

- Use the map to play number and counting games as well: "Can you find three 2s?" "What is the route number on this road?" "How many rivers are in this state?"

- As part of getting ready for a long trip, involve your child in finding and counting things that should be packed — two shirts, three pairs of socks, five books, and so forth.

Show children that you use math skills by "thinking out loud" as you do things such as measuring distances on a map: "Let's see, it's five kilometers to Gurgoan and then three kilometers from Gurgaon to Noida, so that's a total of eight kilometers. It's two kilometers from Gurgaon to Ghaziabad, so that's a total of seven kilometers. Noida is further away from Gurgaon than Ghaziabad is."

2. Are we there Yet?

Grade 1-2

Traveling — whether by car, bus, train or plane — provides many opportunities for children to use mental math and estimation to solve time and distance problems.

What Parents Need?

- Information about how far you're traveling and how long it will take
- Bus, train, or plane schedule

What Can Parents Do?

- On a routine trip around town, point out the time on a watch and say, for example, "It's 3:15, and it takes us 30 minutes to get to your dentist's office. Are we going to get there before your 4:15 appointment?"

- Show your child a bus, train, or plane schedule and explain what it is and how to read it. Point out, for example, that a schedule shows when the bus leaves one place and when it arrives at another. Have him/her figure out how long it takes the bus to get to several places listed on the schedule.

- On a longer trip, occasionally ask your child to estimate how far you've traveled and how much longer it will take to get where you're going. Use road signs or schedules and timetables to help him/her check the answers.

Children develop positive attitudes towards math when they see that their parents and families value it. Find ways to show that you enjoy math. Let your child see you using math not only for routine activities, such as paying bills and following recipes, but also for fun, by playing number games and solving math puzzles.

3. Number Search

Grade 2-3

Traveling provides children with lots of opportunities to practice number recognition as well as counting skills.

What Parents Need?

- Paper
- Crayons or markers
- Ruler

What Can Parents Do?

- Before you leave on a car trip, draw a "Number Search" grid, with five boxes across and 10 boxes down. In each box (moving across from the first box), write a number from 1 to 50. Make a copy of the grid for each family member (except, of course, the driver).

- As you travel, have family members play "Number Search." Tell everyone to be on the lookout for numbers and when they see one on a car or truck, a billboard, a sign, a building, or anything else, to point out the number, then circle it on the grid. (Only the person who spots the number first gets to circle it). The first person to circle all the numbers on the grid wins.

- Ask your child to look for words and phrases on signs and billboards that have numbers (or number words) in them, such as "1-stop shopping," "2-day service," "buy one, get one free" and "open 24 × 7."

Helping children practice number recognition can take many forms. Encourage them to listen for common expressions that include numbers and number words, such as: "Two's company, three's a crowd"; "Two can play that game"; or "Three strikes and you're out."

4. License Plate Riddles

Grades 2-4

License plates can be used both to help children develop their knowledge of numbers and as an introduction to algebra.

What Parents Need?

- License plates
- Paper
- Crayons or markers

What Can Parents Do?

- If you're stuck in traffic, point out the license plate of a car in front of you and ask all family members (except the driver, of course!) to study it closely. Then tell everyone to use the individual numbers on the plate to make the largest three-digit number possible and write it down. For example, if the plate number is 254–116, the largest three-digit number that can be made is 654. Have each person read aloud his or her number. The person with the largest number wins the round. You can change the game by asking everyone to make the smallest three-digit number.

- For your younger child, these activities can be simplified by having them find the largest single or double digit, or even to recognize individual numbers or add all the numbers on the plate.

- Choose a license plate number, for example, 663M218. Then ask your child to use numbers from the plate to solve math problems. Helping children practice number recognition can take many forms, such as the following:

  - add two numbers to get the answer 5.
    [answer: 3+2 = 5]

  - use three numbers to get 5.
    [answer: (3+2) × 1 = 5]

  - use four numbers to get 5.
    [answer: (6+3+1) ÷ 2 = 5]

  - use five numbers to get 5.
    [answer: (6+6+3) - (8+2) = 5]

-    use six numbers to get 5.

[answer: (6+6) + (3×1) - (8+2) = 5]

For fun, point out license plates on which number are part of a message: ALL 41; IML8 (I'm late).

5. License Plate Special

Grades 2-4

License plates can be used to reinforce children's understanding of the language of mathematics as well as their mathematical reasoning abilities.

What Parents Need?

- License plates
- Paper
- Crayons or markers
- Ruler

What Can Parents Do?

- As you travel in a car or on a bus with your child, point out a license plate and read it to him using only number names (excluding the letters). For example, if the license plate is 663M218, read it as six lakhs sixty-three thousands two hundred and eighteen. Ask your child to find and read another license plate. Ask him if his number is less than, greater than or equal to yours.

- Ask your older child to estimate the difference between his number and another license plate number. Is the difference less than 10, more than 100, more than 1,000?

- Ask your child to write the names of the different states he/she sees on license plates (later he/she can check an atlas or dictionary for spellings — or you can help him by using the abbreviations for each state). After the trip, ask him to tell you which state plates he/she saw most often. Which the least often? Help him to make a bar graph to show his findings.

It's important to help children to understand that numbers have the same value whether they are expressed in figures (1, 2, 3) or in words (one, two, three).

6. Ease on Down the Road

Grades 3-5

An important mathematical concept for children to learn is the relationship between two quantities such as *kilometers* per *hour* or *cost* per *litre*.

What Parents Need?

- Maps
- Marker
- Paper and pencil or pen

What Can Parents Do?

On car trips with your child — short or long — take advantage of the following opportunities that allow him to apply his math skills:

- Before leaving on a trip, give him/her a map and tell him/her that you want him/her to be your "navigator" as you drive. Help him/her to mark the route that you will take. Then show him/her how to use distance numbers on the map to estimate the distances between different locations. Check the odometer before you begin the trip and have him/her write down the mileage.

- As you're driving, ask him/her to check the route marked on the map and let you know in advance when you'll need to turn onto another road — the name and about how far away it is. Point out road signs along the way that tell how many kilometers you are from a junction or town or city. Let him point out some for you.

- On the highway, ask your child to read road signs and look for signs that show the speed limits. Then ask him/her to watch the speedometer and let you know if you're driving too fast for the posted limit. Help him/her to practice his/her mental math skills by asking him/her questions such as, "The speed limit is 65 kilometers per hour. How far will we go in one hour? Two hours? three hours? How long will it take us to go 500 kilometers?"

- When you stop for petrol, ask your child to look at the pump to see how many liters of petrol you bought and the cost per litre. If the petrol cost 80 rupees a liter, ask your child what five litres will cost. 10 litres? 20 litres? Ask him if he/she knows an easy way to figure this out. (*estimating the cost by rounding the cost per litre to 80 rupees*)

- When you reach your destination, have your child write down the new mileage on your odometer. Show him/her how to figure the actual number of kilometers you traveled by subtracting the mileage when you left home from the new number. Then have him/her compare the actual mileage to the estimated mileage.

Involving children in planning trips and in giving them important jobs on the trip, such as following the correct route, can increase their self-confidence as well as their math skills. However, if they make mistakes, such as giving the wrong direction for a turn, they need to be reassured that mistakes are part of learning. Help them to understand what went wrong and how to get back on track.

✗ ✗ ✗

MATHEMATICS FOR THE FUN OF IT

"What can you do to promote world peace? Go home
and love your family."
~*Mother Teresa*

During summer vacations, on rainy days, while waiting at the doctor's clinic or on a walk through the neighbourhood, learning never ends. Children can explore some fascinating mathematical possibilities in the world around them every day. For instance, math can be found outdoors in nature: Look for symmetry in leaves; count the number, sizes, and kinds of trees on your street; and look at the various shapes and patterns of blooming flowers. Children will be learning math and enjoying it, too! The activities in this section can be done anywhere.

1. A Tower of Numbers

Pre-school

Playing with blocks is fun, but it also can teach basic math skills such as number recognition, counting, identifying patterns, recognizing symmetry, and sorting.

What Parents Need?

- Sets of blocks that show both numbers (1–10) and letters (at least A to J)

What Can Parents Do?

- Give your child the blocks and tell him/her to sort them so that one set shows numbers and one set shows letters.

- Tell your child to look at the number blocks and choose the block with the number 1. Then have him/her build a tower by choosing and placing the remaining number blocks in the correct order. Have him/her say the name of each number as she places the block.

- Ask your child to build a second tower beside the first using only the letter blocks (beginning with "A") and placing them in order. Have him/her say the name of each letter as he/she places the block.

- Let him/her knock over the towers and scatter the blocks in front of him/her. Then tell him/her to use all the blocks to build a really big tower. When it's finished, have him/her find and point to numbers and letters as you say the names.

- Ask your child to use the blocks to make the following patterns:

    - one number, two letters
    - one letter, one number, two letters
    - A, 5, B, 4, C, 3
    - 1, 2, E, F

Young children can easily confuse letters and numbers. Throughout the day, have them notice and name both, or ask questions such as, "See the sign on that bus. Does it say 5 or E?"

2. Count It Out

Pre-school - Kindergarten

Counting games make developing number sense easy and fun.

What Parents Need?

- A group of 20–25 counters (beads, blocks, plastic eggs, coins), with three or four counters different from the others in some way (for example, red beads in a group of blue beads; coins in a group of one rupee coins)

- Dice

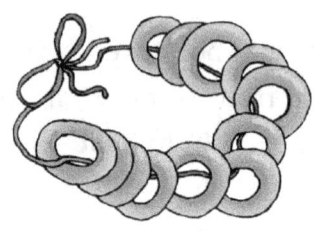

What Can Parents Do?

- Sit on the floor with your child and arrange the counters in a circle between you. Have him/her toss the dice and say the number that comes up. Tell him/her to start at any point in the circle — except for one of the counters that is "different" — and count to that number, touching each counter as he/she goes.

- If he/she stops on a "regular" counter (a blue bead), he/she gets to take the counter and have another turn. If he/she stops on the different counter (the red bead), you get a turn. Leave the different counter in the circle.

- The winner is the player with the most counters when only the different counters remain. Involve the family and expand the game!

Be sure to use counters that are small enough for small hands to move but large enough not to pose a choking hazard.

3. Guess what I'm Thinking

Kindergarten-Grade 2

Games give children a chance to use math skills and math language in a non-threatening situation.

What Parents Do?

- Let your child think of a number within a range of numbers. Try to guess the number by asking him/her questions. Here's a sample:

(for kindergarten children)

> Child: I am thinking of a number between 1 and 10.
>
> Parent: Is it more than 6?
>
> Child: No.
>
> Parent: Is it less than 3?
>
> Child: No.
>
> *(The child could be thinking of 4 or 5)*

(for first and second graders)

> Child: I am thinking of a number between 1 and 100.
>
> Parent: Is it more than 50?

Child: No.

Parent: Is it an even number?

Child: No.

Parent: Is it more than 20 but less than 40?

Child: Yes.

Parent: Can you reach it by starting at 20 and counting by 5s?

Child: Yes.

(The child could be thinking of 25, 30, or 35)

- After you've guessed your child's number, let him/her guess a number that you're thinking of by asking similar questions.

It is important to help children in developing an understanding of the characteristics of numbers — such as odd and even — and meanings of terms such as "more than" and "less than".

4. Open for Business

Grades 1-5

Learning to use a calculator can help children understand and apply estimation and mathematical reasoning skills, as well as learn addition, subtraction, division, and multiplication.

What Parents Need?

- Empty containers (cartons or boxes)
- Old magazines, books, newspapers
- Calculator
- Pencil or crayon
- Paper

What Can Parents Do?

- Help your child collect empty containers so that you can play as if you were shopping at the grocery store. Gather the items and put them on a table. Help think of a price for each item. Mark the prices on the containers. You can even mark some items on sale.

- Pretend to be the customer while your child is the cashier. Ask questions such as the following:
  - How much would it cost to buy three trays of eggs?
  - If the price of soap is 50 rupees for two bars, then how much does one bar of soap cost?

- If I don't buy the cereal, how much is my bill?

- How much more will it cost if I buy this magazine?

• Show your older child how math symbols (for example, +, -, ÷, x and =) are used on a calculator. Help him/her add the prices of each item on the calculator and total the amount using the (=) symbol. Have him/her write the total on a piece of paper, which will be your receipt.

• Have your child estimate the total cost of the items you are buying. Have him/her use a calculator to see if his/her estimate is correct.

Learning to use calculators is important for children — they're part of everyday life. However, they have no replacement for strong arithmetic, children should not be encouraged to rely too heavily on calculators.

5. What Coins do I Have?

Grades 2-5

Using mathematical reasoning skills to figure out the unknown is good preparation for understanding algebra.

What Parents Need?

- Coins of different denominations

- Paper

- Pen or pencil

What Can Parents Do?

- Choose coins so that your child can't see, then hold out your closed hand and ask him/her questions such as the following:

   - I have three coins in my hand. They're worth 7 rupees. What coins do I have? *(1 five rupee coin and 2 one rupee coins)*

   - I have three coins in my hand. They're worth 16 rupees. What coins do I have? *(a ten rupee coin, a five rupee coin, 1 one rupee coin)*

   - I have three coins in my hand. They're worth 11 rupees. What coins do I have? *(2 five rupee coins and 1 one rupee coin)*

   - I have three coins in my hand. They're worth 30 rupees. What coins do I have? *(3 ten rupee coins) Ask your child to tell you how he/she knows the answer.*

- Make the game more challenging by asking questions that have more than one answer:

   - I have six coins in my hand. They're worth 30 rupees. What coins could I have? *(6 five rupee coins).*

- I have coins in my hand that are worth 11 rupees. How many coins could I have? *(1 one rupee coin and 1 ten rupee coin; 1 one rupee coin and 2 five rupee coins; all one rupee coins) Again, ask your child to tell you how he/she knows the answer.*

You get the idea! Give your child coins to figure out the answers.

Games that involve math should be fun for children, so keep it light!

6. What are My Chances?

Grades 2-5

Playing games that involve chance is one way to introduce children to the meaning of probability.

What Parents Need?

- Two coins
- Paper and pencil

What Can Parents Do?

Play these coin games with your child:

- *Flip one coin.* Every time it comes up heads, your child gets 1 point. Every time it comes up tails, you get 1 point. Flip it 50 times. Tally by 5s to make it easier to keep track of scores. The player with the most points wins. If one player has 10 points more than the other person does, he/she scores an extra 10 points. Ask your child to notice how often this happens. *(Not very often!)*

- *Flip two coins.* If the coins come up two tails or two heads, your child scores 1 point. If it comes up heads and tails, you get 1 point. After 50 flips, see who has more points. Ask your child if he/she thinks this game is fair. What would happen if one player received 2 points for every double heads and the other player received 1 point for everything else. Would that be fair?

- *Flip another coin.* Then flip the other. If the second coin matches the first coin, your child scores 1 point. If the second coin doesn't match the first coin, you receive 1 point. Try this 50 times. Is the result same as in the previous game?

Call attention to the role that probability plays in everyday life by pointing out how it is used in TV weather forecasts or sports stories.

7. Card Smarts

Variations for all Grades

Games with number cards can help children develop strategies for using numbers in different combinations by adding, subtracting, multiplying and dividing.

What Parents Need?

- Sets of number cards, 1–10 (you can make your own using heavy paper or index cards)

- Pencil and paper

- Coin

What Can Parents Do?

Here are some games that you and your child can play with number cards:

- *Number Sandwich*: With your younger child, review the numbers 1 to 10. Make sure that he/she knows the correct order of the numbers. Sit with him/her and shuffle and place two sets of number cards in a pile between you. Have him/her draw two cards from the pile and arrange them in order in front of him/her, for example 3 and 6, leaving a space between. Then have him/her draw a third card. Ask him/her where the card should be placed to be in the right order — in the middle? before the 3? after the 6?

- *More or Less:* Sit with your young child and place a shuffled set of number cards between you. Flip the coin and have your child call "heads" or "tails" to see if the winner of each round will be the person with a greater value card (heads) or a smaller value card (tails). Then each of you will draw a card. Compare the cards to see who wins that round. Continue through all the cards. When your child is comfortable with this game, change it just a bit. Divide the cards evenly between the two of you. Each of you places the cards face down and turns over one card at the same time. Have your child compare the cards to see if his card is more or less than yours. If his card is more than yours, ask him how much more. If it is less, ask how much less. The player with the greater or smaller value card (depending on whether heads or tails was tossed) takes both cards. The winner of the game is the player with more cards when all the cards have been used.

- *Make a Number:* This game is for your older child and can be played with family and friends. Give each player a piece of paper and a pencil. Deal each player four number cards with the numbers showing. Explain that, using all four cards and a choice of any combination of addition, subtraction, multiplication, and division the player must make as many different numbers as possible in two minutes. The player gets one point for each answer.

Encourage children to use number cards to make up their own games for the family to play.

8. Calculated Answers

Variations for All Grades

Learning to use the special functions of calculators can expand children's knowledge of many arithmetic operations, help them to recognize number patterns and increase their ability to reason mathematically.

What Parents Need?

- Calculator with counting function

What Can Parents Do?

- Give your child a calculator that is appropriate for his/her age (one with large, easy-to-read keys is especially helpful). Show him how he/ she can make the calculator "count" in sequence for him. (For most calculators, this is done by pushing a number button, then the + sign, then the button for the number to be added, then the = sign: for example: 1 + 1 =. To make the calculator count in sequence by adding 1, keep pushing the = button: 1 + 1 = 2 . . . 3. . . 4 . . . 5 and so on). Give the calculator to your child and have him/her try this, starting with 1 + 1.

- When your child is comfortable with this function, have him/her explore number patterns such as 2 + 2 =, 5 + 5 =, 50 + 50 =, and so forth.

- Next, show your child that he/she can use the same procedure to subtract — by substituting the − sign for the + sign: 50 − 1 =, or 100 − 5 = . Encourage him/her to explore other patterns.

- Let your older child learn about negative numbers by seeing what the calculator shows when they count down from 0 (for example, 0 − 2 = 2).

- Create number pattern puzzles for your child to solve. Try the following:

    - Write a sequence of numbers that follows a pattern, such as 3, 6, 9, 12. Ask your child what number comes next. Have him/her explain what the pattern is (*counting by 3s*).

- Have your older child fill in missing numbers in patterns, such as 43, 38, _____, _____, 23, _____, 13. Ask him/her what the pattern is.

  (*subtracting by 5s*)

- Have your child create number patterns for you to identify.

Asking children to explain in their own words how they arrive at a solution to a problem — including how they used a calculator — encourages them to get into the habit of thinking and reasoning mathematically.

✘✘✘

Always kiss your
children goodnight,
even if they're already
asleep.

~H. Jackson Brown, Jr.

GLOSSARY

> "Parenting now is a two-way relationship where you
> learn from each other."
> *~Juhi Chawla*

Algebra: A form of advanced arithmetic in which letters of the alphabet represent unknown numbers. Children use simple algebra when they solve a problem such as 4 + ? = 7 (a problem they would phrase as "4 + x = 7" when they get older and begin to study algebra).

Arithmetic: A branch of mathematics taught to youngsters in elementary school. It deals with numbers and how to use them in the operations of addition, subtraction, multiplication, and division.

Classification: Identifying ways in which objects are similar (such as colour, size, or shape).

Geometry: A branch of mathematics that deals with measurement, properties and relationships of points, lines, angles, surfaces, and solids. For young children, geometry begins by recognizing shapes and patterns; formal study begins later.

Mathematical Reasoning: Thinking through math problems logically in order to arrive at solutions. It involves being able to identify what is important and unimportant in solving a problem and to explain or justify a solution.

Measurement: Determining the length, area, volume, time, and other quantities and using the appropriate tools to do so. Units of measure include inches, feet, grams, kilograms, tons, gallons, litres, rupees.

Number Sense: The ability to recognize numbers, identify their relative values and understand how to use them in a variety of ways, such as counting, measuring, or estimating.

Probability: The chance that a given event will occur. It is an important area of mathematics study and a subject to which young children can be introduced through games of chance, such as coin tosses.

Statistics and
Data Analysis: The collection and analysis of numerical data. Counting people in a census is a statistical activity. So is computing a batting average or figuring the miles per gallon that your car averages on a trip.

Symmetry: The property of an object when the characteristics (size, shape, and relative position of parts) are the same on either side of a dividing line or about a center.

✗✗✗

HAPPINESS is WHEN...

YOU REALIZE YOUR CHILDREN HAVE TURNED OUT TO BE GOOD PEOPLE.

WHAT DOES EFFECTIVE MATHEMATICS INSTRUCTION LOOK LIKE?

"The real property that a parent can transmit to all equally is his or her character and educational facilities."
~*Mahatma Gandhi*

As a result of recent efforts to strengthen the mathematics curricula in our nation's schools, from basic through more advanced levels, the instruction that you can see in your child's mathematics classes may look quite a bit different from what you experienced when you were in elementary school. For instance, in effective math classrooms today, you can see the following:

Children are expected to know both basic arithmetic skills and the mathematical concepts that are the bases of these skills: They are learning and applying basic computational skills, and they will also be learning that mathematics is much more than knowing the "facts" and number operations. Young children are learning arithmetic — addition, subtraction, multiplication, and division — and they also are using mathematical operations such as counting, measuring, weighing, reading charts, graphs and identifying patterns and shapes. Across the grades, children are practising the use of their mathematics' skills in many different ways, and they are using the language of math to talk about what they're doing. They are using mathematical operations that involve estimation, geometry, probability, statistics, and the ability to interpret mathematical information. As they progress through school, children will increasingly show that they understand why they are using a particular math skill, recognize when they've made procedural errors and know what to do to correct those errors.

Children are involved actively in the study of mathematics: They are doing tasks that involve investigation, application, and interpretation. They are talking about and writing explanations for their mathematical reasoning.

Children sometimes are working with one another: They sometimes collaborate to make discoveries, draw conclusions, and discuss mathematical concepts and operations.

Children are striving to achieve high standards and are assessed regularly to determine their progress: The government calls for all children to be taught math by teachers who have the training needed to teach effectively, using curricula that are grounded in scientifically based research. The law requires annual math assessments of students in grades 3–8 according to state-defined standards and dissemination of the results to parents, teachers, principals, and others. Curriculum based on state standards should be taught in the classroom; thus assessment would be aligned with instruction. In addition to assessments required by the government, teachers are using many different ways to determine if children know and understand mathematics concepts. Some of these ways are open-ended questions in which a student writes out the steps or thought processes — used in solving a math problem; independent projects and other written tests.

Children are learning to use calculators appropriately: They are using calculators not as crutches but as tools for performing operations with large numbers. **Use of a calculator will not replace a thorough knowledge of basic mathematical operations.**

Children are using computers appropriately:
They are using computers to run software that pose interesting problem situations that would not be available to them without the use of technology.

✘ ✘ ✘

Listen to the desires of your children.
Encourage them and then give them
the autonomy to make their own decision.
~ Denis Waitley

HELPING YOUR CHILD SUCCEED AS A MATHEMATICS STUDENT

"Let us Sacrifice our Today so that our Children can
have Better Tomorrow."
~APJ Abdul Kalam

H ere are some things that you can do to help your
child be a successful mathematics student:

Visit your child's school: Meet with his/her
teacher and ask how your child approaches mathematics.
Does he/she enjoy it? Does he/she participate actively?
Does he/she understand assignments and do them
accurately? If the teacher indicates that your child has
problems with math, ask for specific things that you can
to help him/her.

Check math homework and other assignments: It's indeed a good idea to check that your younger child has finished his/her math homework assignments. If your older child is having trouble in finishing assignments, check his/her work, too. After your child's teacher returns math homework, have your child bring it home so that you can read the comments to see if he/she has done the assignment satisfactorily. *However, do not do homework for your child!* Limit your assistance to seeing that your child understands the assignments and that he/she has the necessary supplies to do them. Too much parental involvement in homework can make children dependent — and take away from the value of homework as a way for children to become independent and responsible.

Find out whether your child's teacher is highly qualified and whether the school follows state standards for mathematics instruction. Ask the school principal for a school handbook or math curriculum guide. If your school doesn't have a handbook, ask the principal and teachers questions such as the following:

- What math teaching methods and materials are used? Are the methods used to teach math based on scientific evidence about what works best? Are the materials up to date?

- How much time is spent on math instruction?

- How does the school measure student progress in math? What tests does it use? How do the students at the school score on state assessments of math?

- Does the school follow state math standards and guidelines?

- Are the math teachers highly qualified? Do they meet state certification and subject-area knowledge requirements?

If you have not seen it, ask to look at the government report card for your school. These report cards show how your school compares to others in the district and indicate how well it is succeeding.

Find out if the school has a website and, if so, get the address: School websites can provide you with ready access to all kinds of information, including homework assignments, class schedules, lesson plans, and dates for school district and state tests.

Help your child by seeing that the mathematics he/she is learning is very much a part of everyday life: From statistics in sports to the sale price of clothing to the amount of petrol needed to travel from one city to another, mathematics is important to us every day. Help your child to link his "school" math to practical events.

Point out that many jobs require mathematical skills: Your child may recognize that many people must have good math skills to do their jobs — scientists, doctors, computer technicians, accountants and bankers, for example. However, he/she may not realize that many other jobs also require mathematical skills. Point out that math also is used in jobs such as running a business; being a mechanical person; being a salesperson or clerk; and designing clothes, or buildings. Let him/her know that having strong math skills will open up many great career opportunities.

Stimulate your child's interest in technology: Help your child learn how to use calculators — but don't let him/her rely solely on them to solve math problems. Encourage him/her to learn to use computers to extend what he/she is learning and to find math games and math-related websites that will increase his/her interest in math.

Show your child that you like mathematics: Letting your child see that you use math and that you aren't afraid of it, will go much further to building positive attitudes than just telling him/her that he/she should learn it.

Set high standards for your child in mathematics' achievement: Challenge your child to succeed in math and encourage his/her interest by doing the kinds of activities suggested in this book and by trying many more activities of your own.

✗ ✗ ✗

THE SOLUTION TO EVERY PARENTING PROBLEM STARTS WITH NINE LITTLE WORDS:
'I'M HERE.'
'I HEAR YOU.'
'HOW CAN I HELP?'

RESOURCES

Websites

- www.aplusmath.com
- www.coolmath4kids.com
- www.funbrain.com/numbers.html
- www.mathleague.com
- www.easymaths.org
- www.mathcats.com
- www.figurethis.org
- www.coolmath.com
- www.AAAmath.com
- www.kidsites.com/sites-edu/math.htm
- www.mathplayground.com
- www.amathsdictionaryforkids.com

- www.kidsnumbers.com
- www.teachrkids.com
- www.allmath.com
- www.math.rice.edu/~lanius/Lessons/
- www.learn4good.com/kids/math.htm
- www.squidoo.com/k12interactivemath
- www.helpwithassignment.blogspot.com/2011/02/online-math-games-for-children-teach.html
- www.teachthechildrenwell.com/math.html

Books for Children

The following is only a sampling of the many available math-related children's books that your child might enjoy. Please ask your local or school librarian to help you to find other appropriate titles. Your librarian can help you to locate books in a particular language.

This list is divided into two groups, those books most appropriate for you to read with your younger child and those that will appeal to your older child, who reads independently. However, you're the best judge of which books are appropriate for your child, regardless of age.

Preschool-Grade 2

- Adler, David A. *Fun with Fractions*. Holiday House.

- Anno, Mitsumasa. *Anno's Math Games*. Philomel Books.

- Axelrod, Amy. *Pigs at Odds: Fun with Math and Games*. Simon and Schuster.

- Brown, Marc. One Two Three: An Animal Counting Book. Little Brown.

- Burns, Marilyn. *The Greedy Triangle* (Brainy Day Books). Scholastic.

- Carle, Eric. *1, 2, 3 to the Zoo*. Philomel Books.

- Dee, Ruby. *Two Ways to Count to Ten*. Holt.

- Demi. *Demi's Count the Animals 1 2 3*. Grosset and Dunlap.

- Feelings, Muriel. *Moja Means One: Swahili Counting Book*. Dial.

- Fox, Mem. *The Straight Line Wonder*. Mondo.

- Greene, Rhonda G. *When a Line Bends, a Shape Begins*. Houghton Mifflin.

- Hoban, Tana. *So Many Circles, So Many Squares*. Greenwillow.

- Hopkins, Lee Bennett. *Marvelous Math: A Book of Poems*. Turtleback Books.

- Hudson, Cheryl Willis. *Afro-Bets 1 2 3 Book*. Just Us Productions.

- Hutchins, Pat. *The Doorbell Rang*. Greenwillow Books.

- Jones, Carol. *This Old Man*. Houghton Mifflin Company.

- Lionni, Leo. *Numbers to Talk About.* Pantheon Books.

- Miller, Jane. *Farm Counting Book.* Aladdin Library.

- Pinczes, Elinor J. *A Remainder of One.* Houghton Mifflin.

- Pluckrose, Henry. *Numbers and Counting: Let's Explore.* Gareth Stevens.

- Schwartz, David M. *How Much Is a Million?* Scholastic

- Scieszka, Jon. *Math Curse.* Viking.

- Tafuri, Nancy. *Who's Counting?* Mulberry Books.

- Ziefert, Harriet. *A Dozen Ducklings Lost and Found: A Counting Story.*

- Houghton Mifflin/Walter Lorraine Books.

Grades 3-5

- Adler, David A. *Shape Up! Fun with Triangles and Other Polygons.* Holiday House.

- Burns, Marilyn. *I Hate Mathematics!* (A Brown Paper School Book). Little, Brown.

- Clement, Rod. *Counting on Frank.* Gareth Stevens.

- Garland, Trudi H. *Fibonacci Fun: Fascinating Activities with Intriguing Numbers.* Dale Seymour Publications.

- Holub, Joan. *Riddle-Iculous Math*. Albert Whitman.

- Julius, Edward K. *Arithmatricks: 50 Easy Ways to Add, Subtract, Multiply and Divide without a Calculator*. John Wiley & Sons.

- Lopresti, Angeline Sparagna. *A Place for Zero: A Math Adventure*. Charlesbridge Publishing.

- Murphy, Stuart J. *Sluggers' Car Wash*. HarperCollins.

- Neuschwander, Cindy. *Circumference and the First Round Table: A Math Adventure*. Charlesbridge Publishing.

- Pappas, Theoni. *Fractals, Googols and Other Mathematical Tales*. Wide World Publishing.

- Peterson, Ivars and Henderson, Nancy. *Math Trek: Adventures in the Math Zone*. John Wiley & Sons.

- Schmandt-Besserat, Denise. *The History of Counting*. HarperCollins.

- Swartz, David M. *G Is for Googol: A Math Alphabet Book*. Triangle Press.

- Tang, Greg. *The Grapes of Math: Mind Stretching Math Riddles*. Scholastic.

- Viorst, Judith. Alexander *Who Used to Be Rich Last Sunday*. Atheneum.

- Wise, Bill. *Whodunit Math Puzzles*. Sterling.

- Zaslavsky, Claudia. *Math Games & Activities From Around the World*. Chicago Review Press.

Math Software

Many Websites provide information and reviews that you can use to select the best mathematics software for your child. Here are just a few of those Websites:

Children's Math Software:

https://education.cu-portland.edu/blog/ classroom-resources/4-math-software- programs-for-kids/

Children's Math Games:

https://en.softonic.com/downloads/math- games-for-kids

Learning Village: **www.learningvillage.com/**

Superkids (the educational software review page): **www.superkids.com**

Understand Your Child: Teen and Child Personality Test

http://www.personalitylab.org/tests/ bfi2_parent_outs.htm

x x x